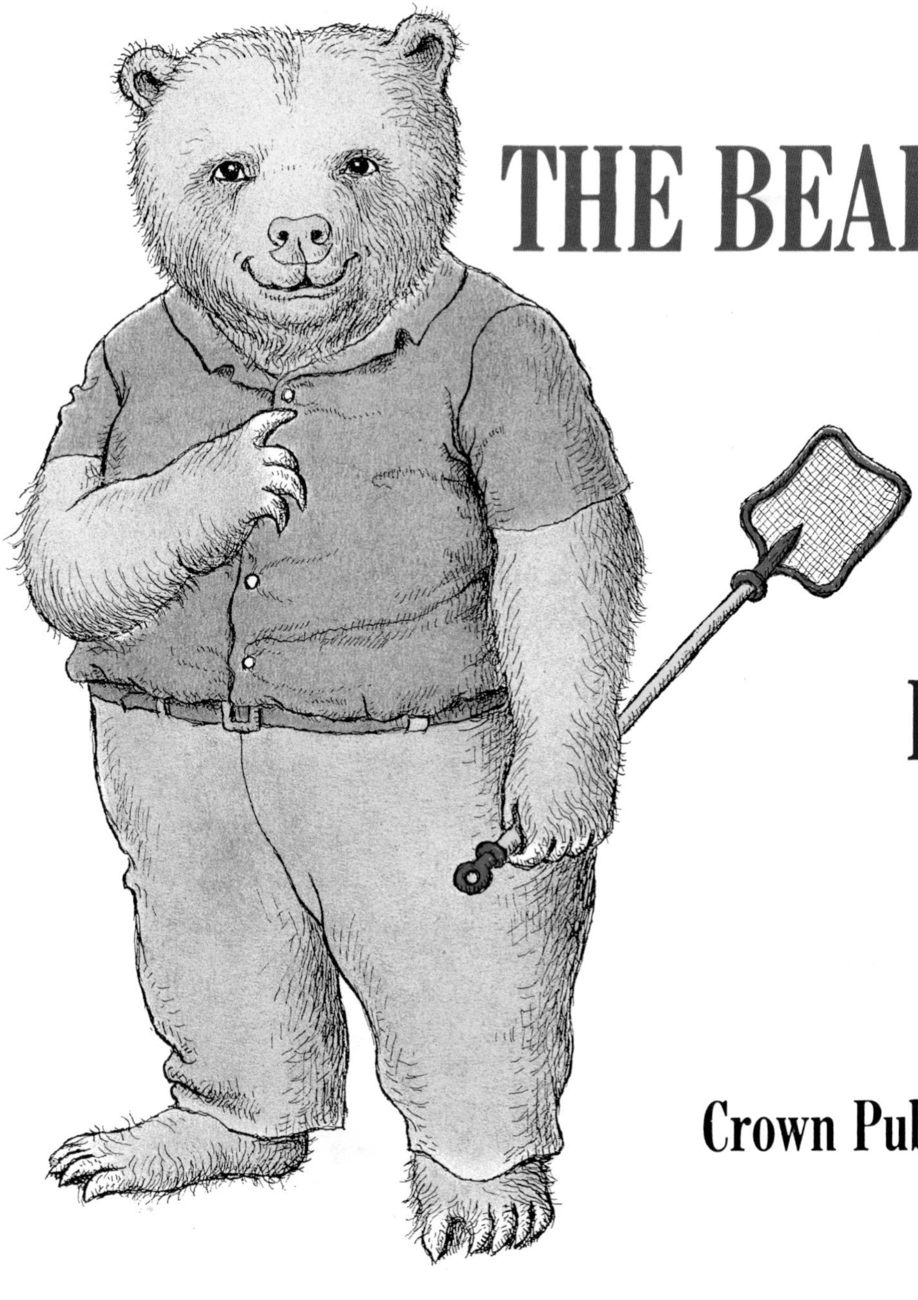

THE BEAR & THE FLY

a story by

PAULA WINTER

Crown Publishers, Inc. New York

Copyright © 1976 by Paula Winter
All rights reserved. No part of this publication may be
reproduced, stored in a retrieval system, or transmitted, in any
form or by any means, electronic, mechanical, photocopying,
recording, or otherwise, without the prior written permission of
the publisher. Published by Crown Publishers, Inc.,
a Random House company,
225 Park Avenue South, New York, New York 10003
CROWN is a trademark of Crown Publishers, Inc.
Manufactured in Hong Kong

Library of Congress Cataloging-in-Publication Data
Winter, Paula.
The bear and the fly.
Summary: A bear tries to catch a fly with
disastrous results.
[1. Bears—Fiction. 2. Stories without
words] I. Title.
PZ7.W762Be   [E]   76-2479
ISBN 0-517-52605-0 (trade)
0-517-56552-8 (pbk.)
10 9 8 7

For Norma Jean

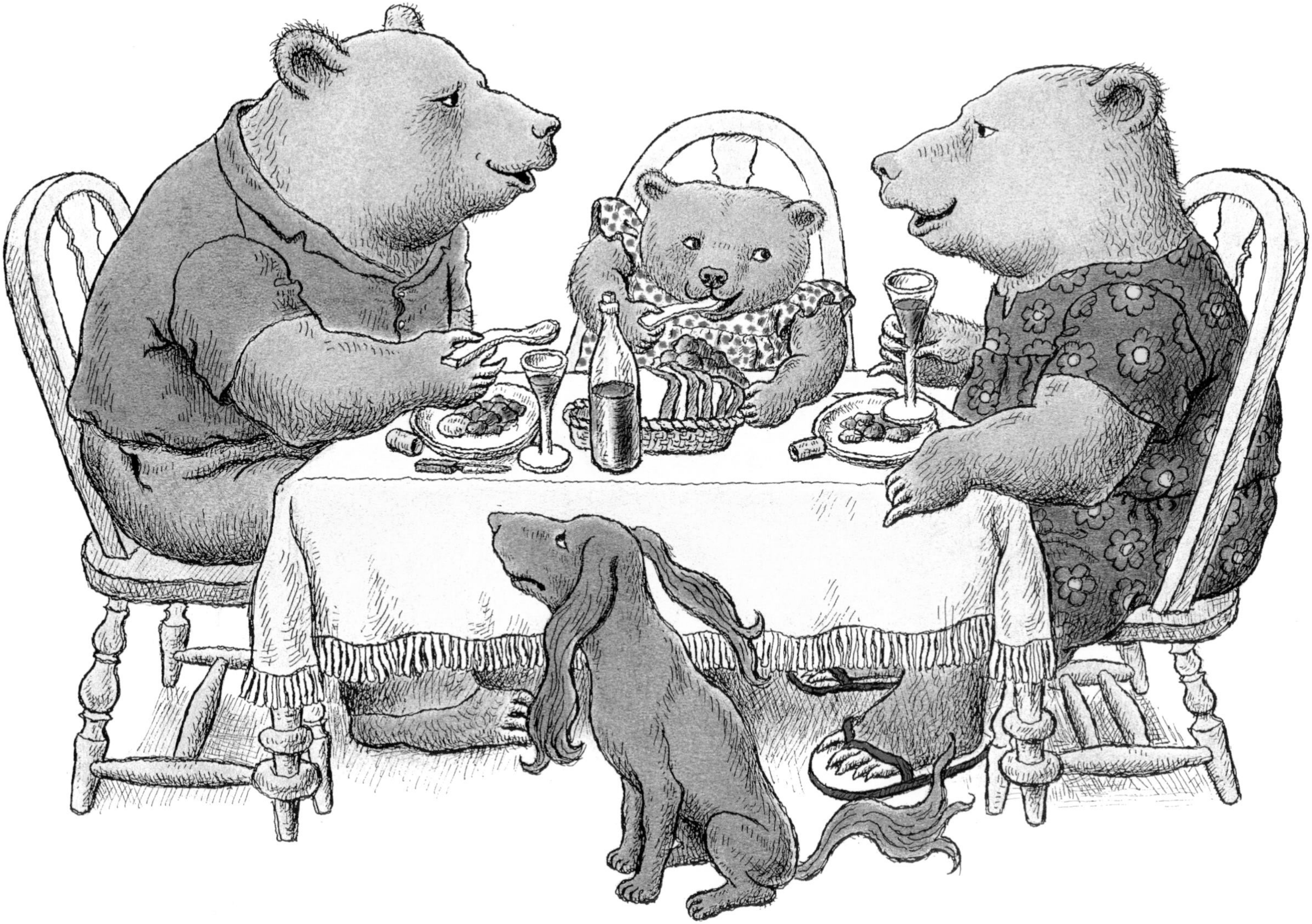

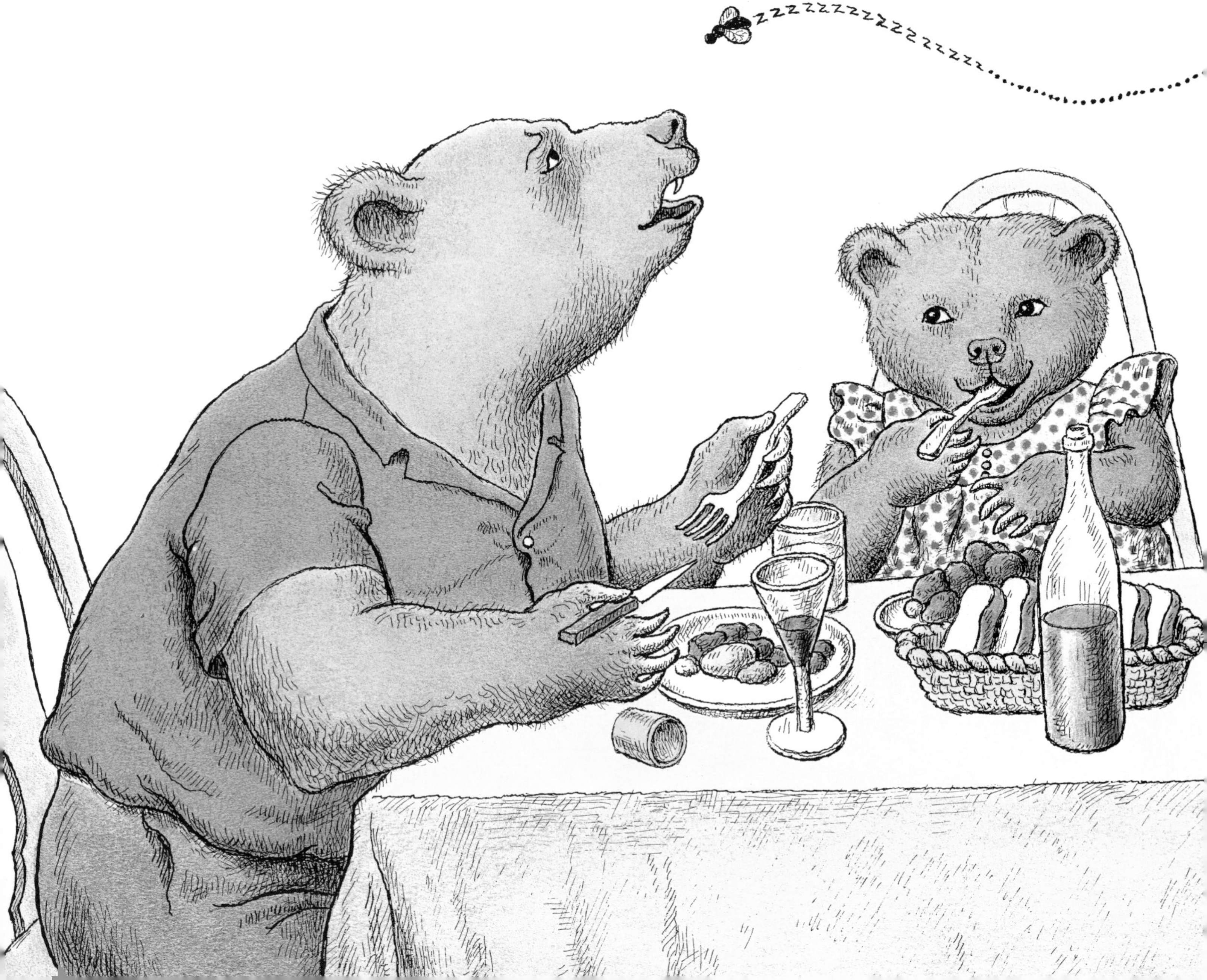
zzzzzzzzzzzzzzzz

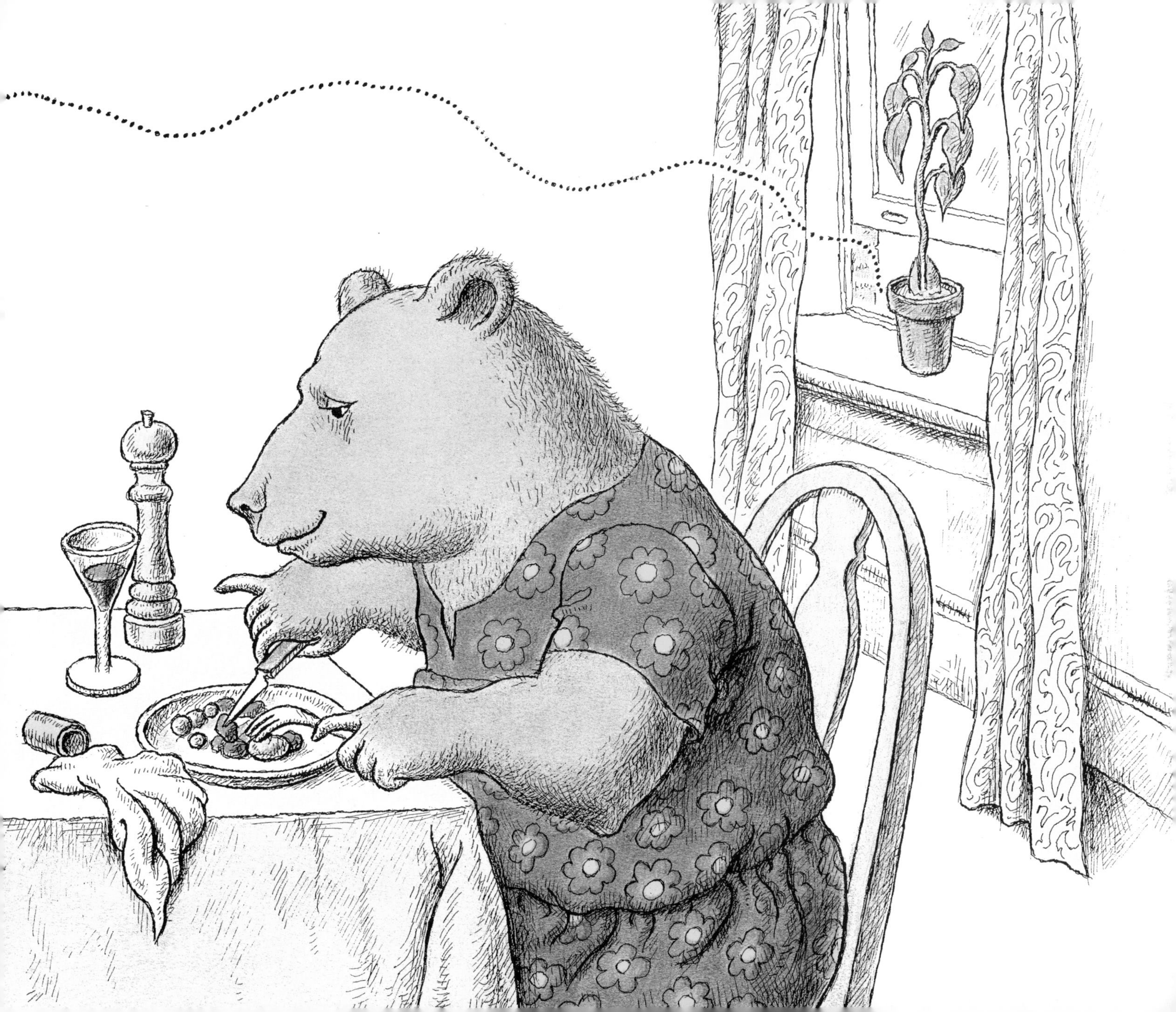

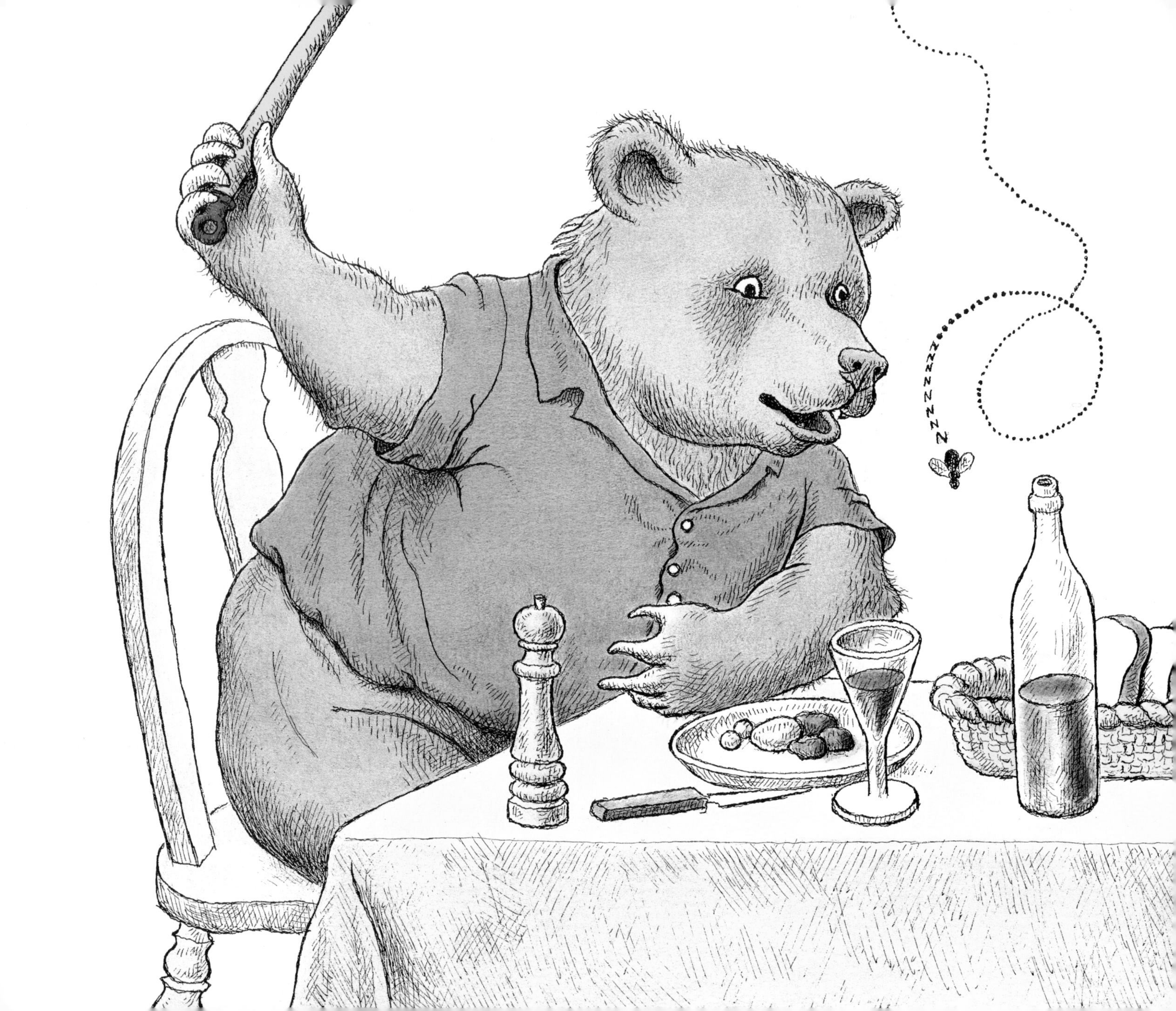

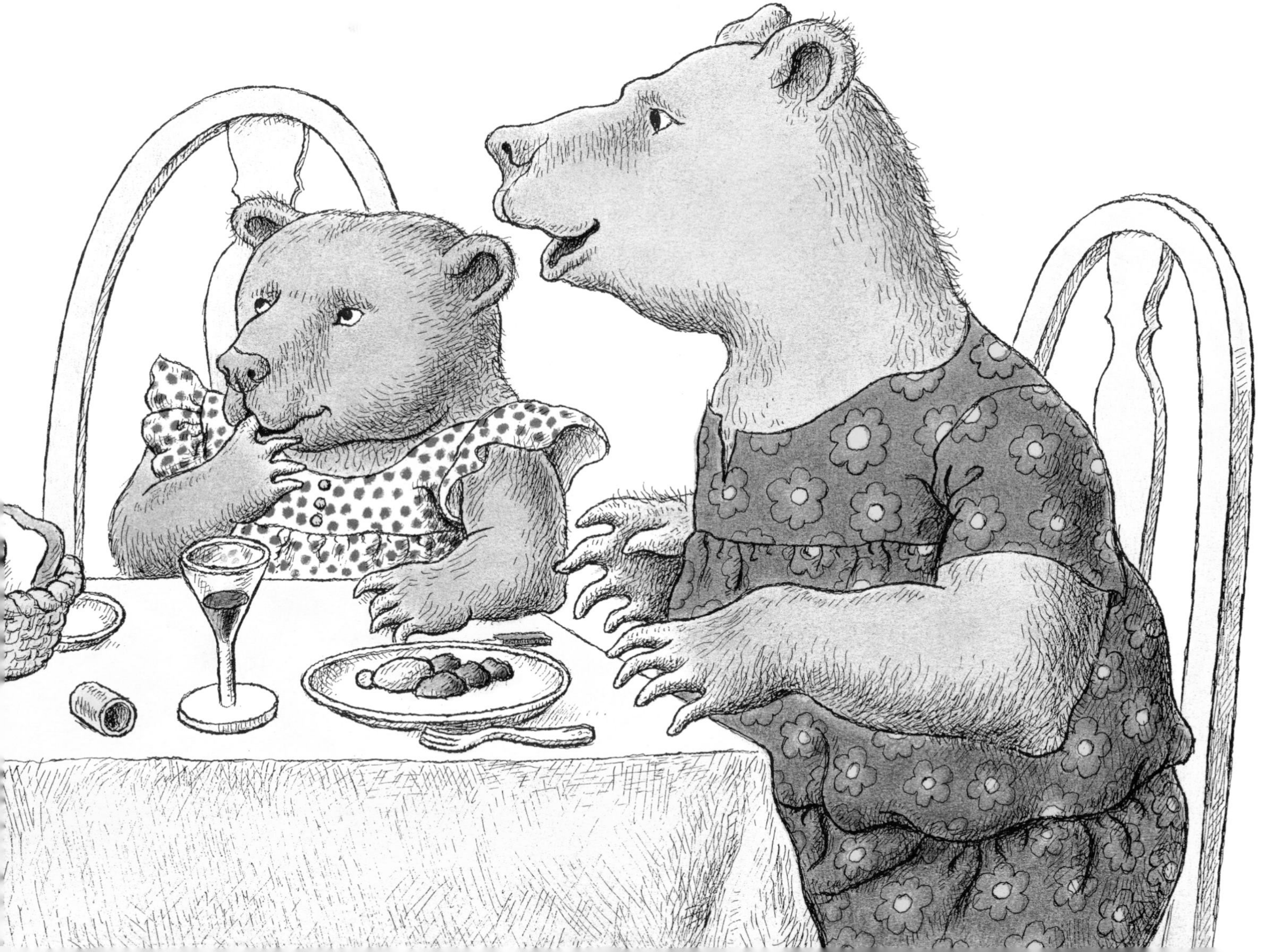

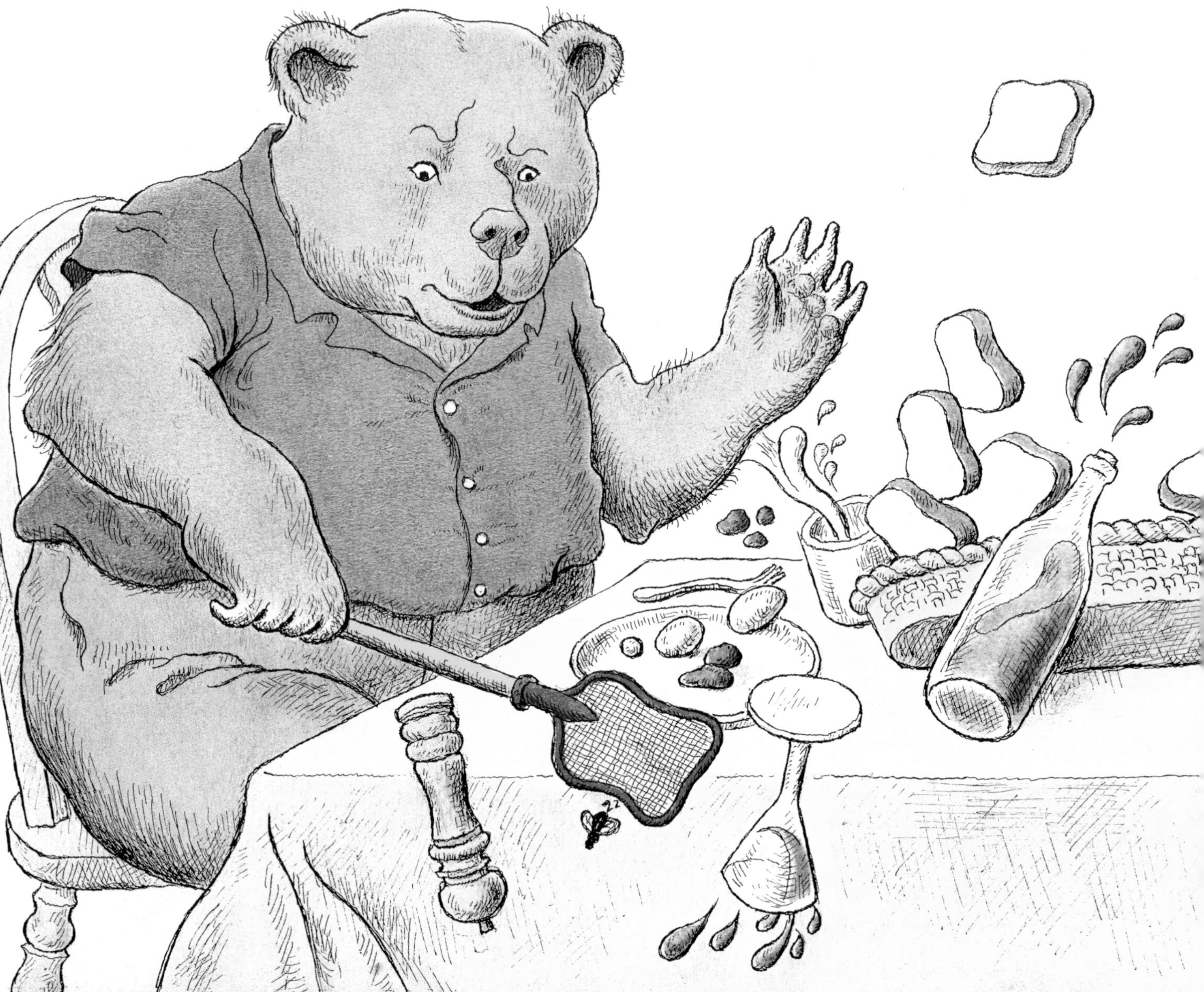

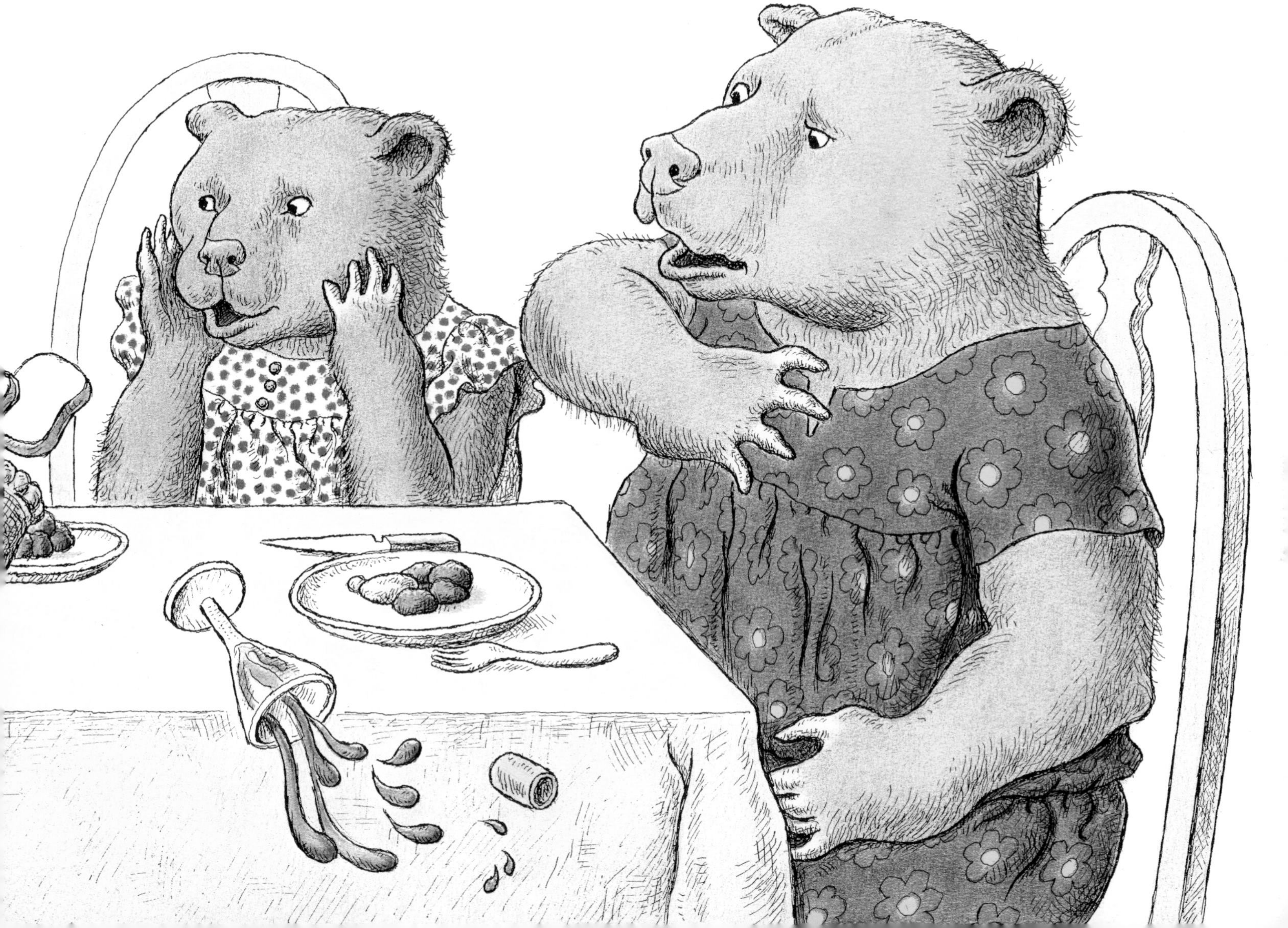

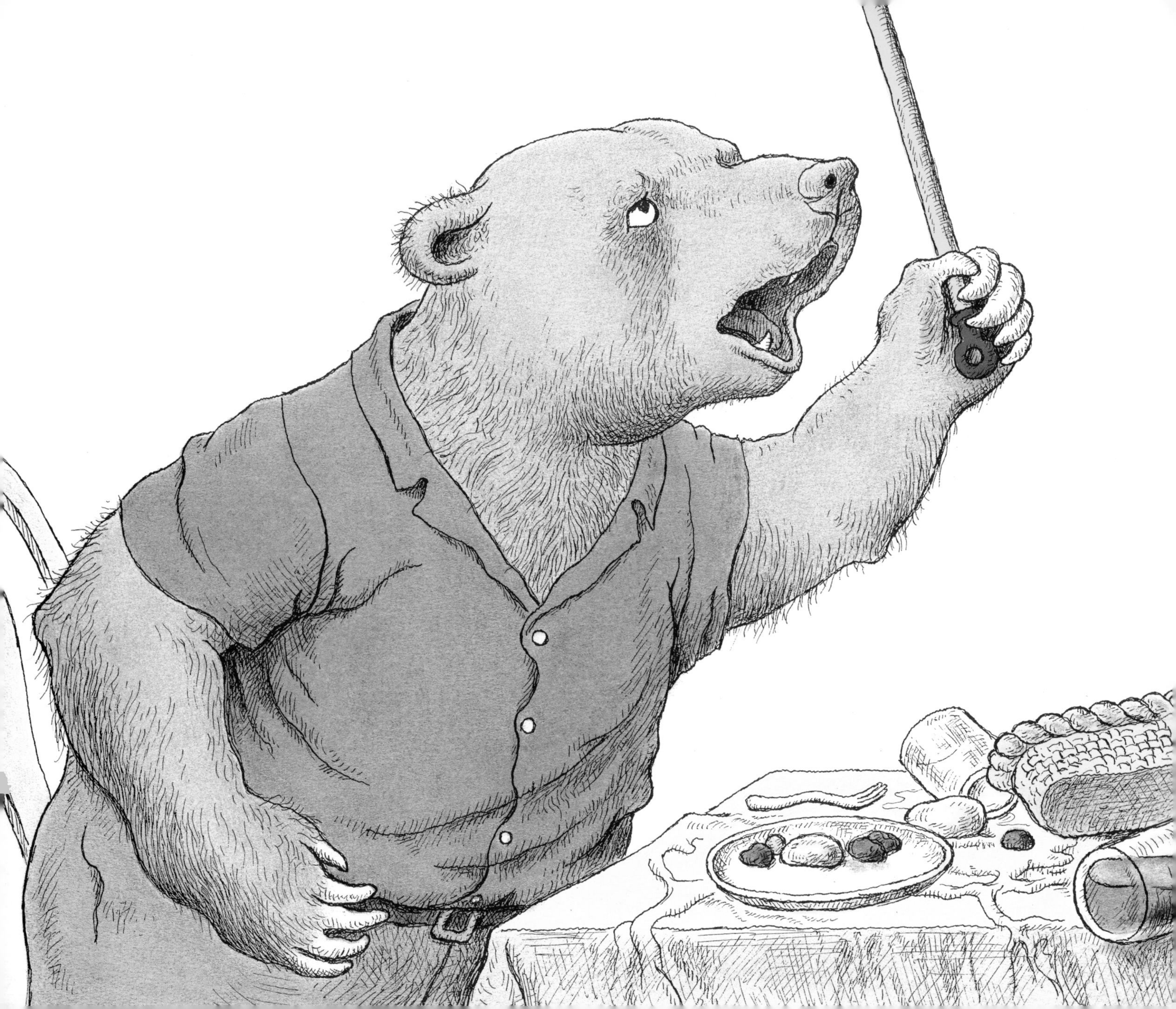

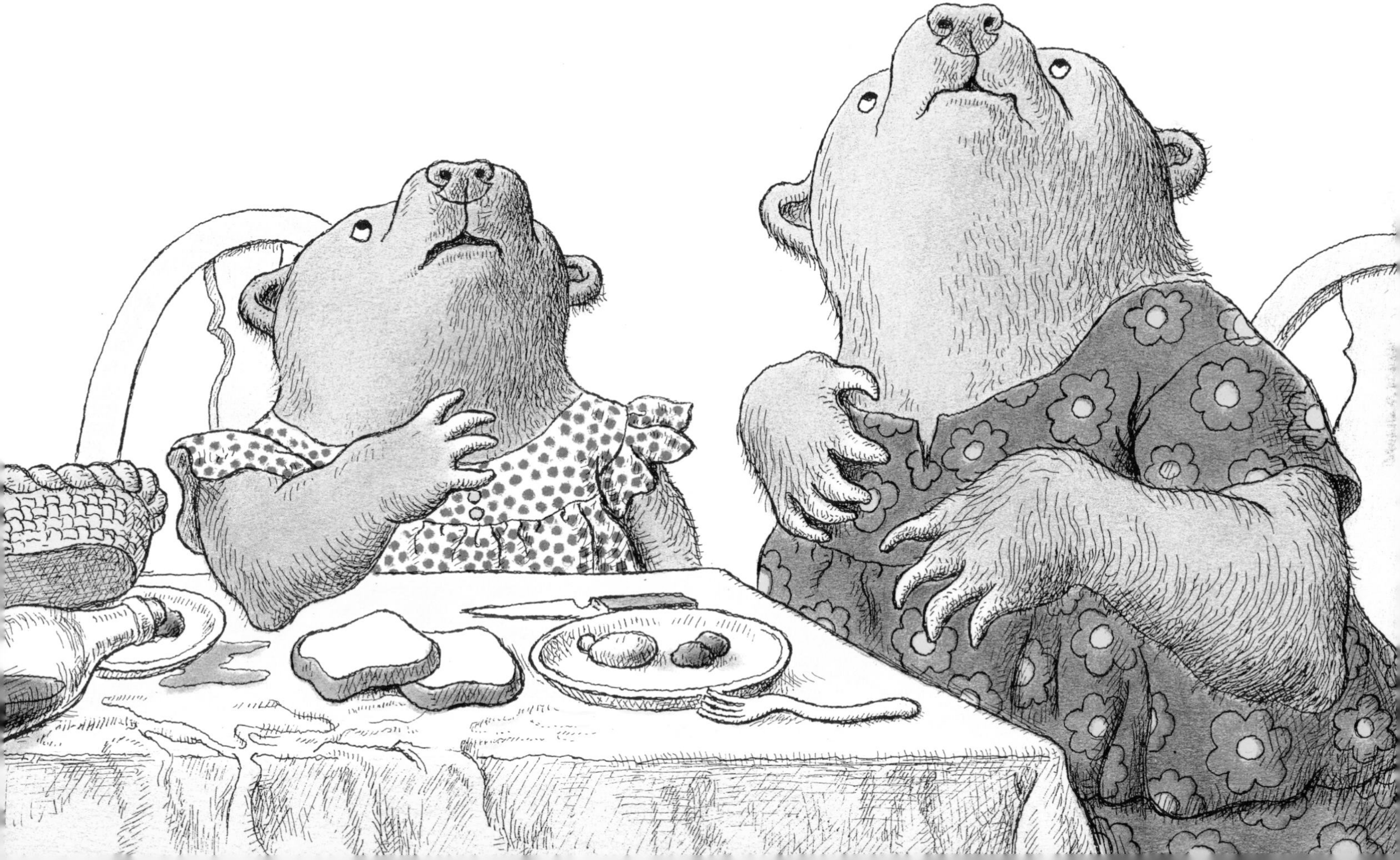

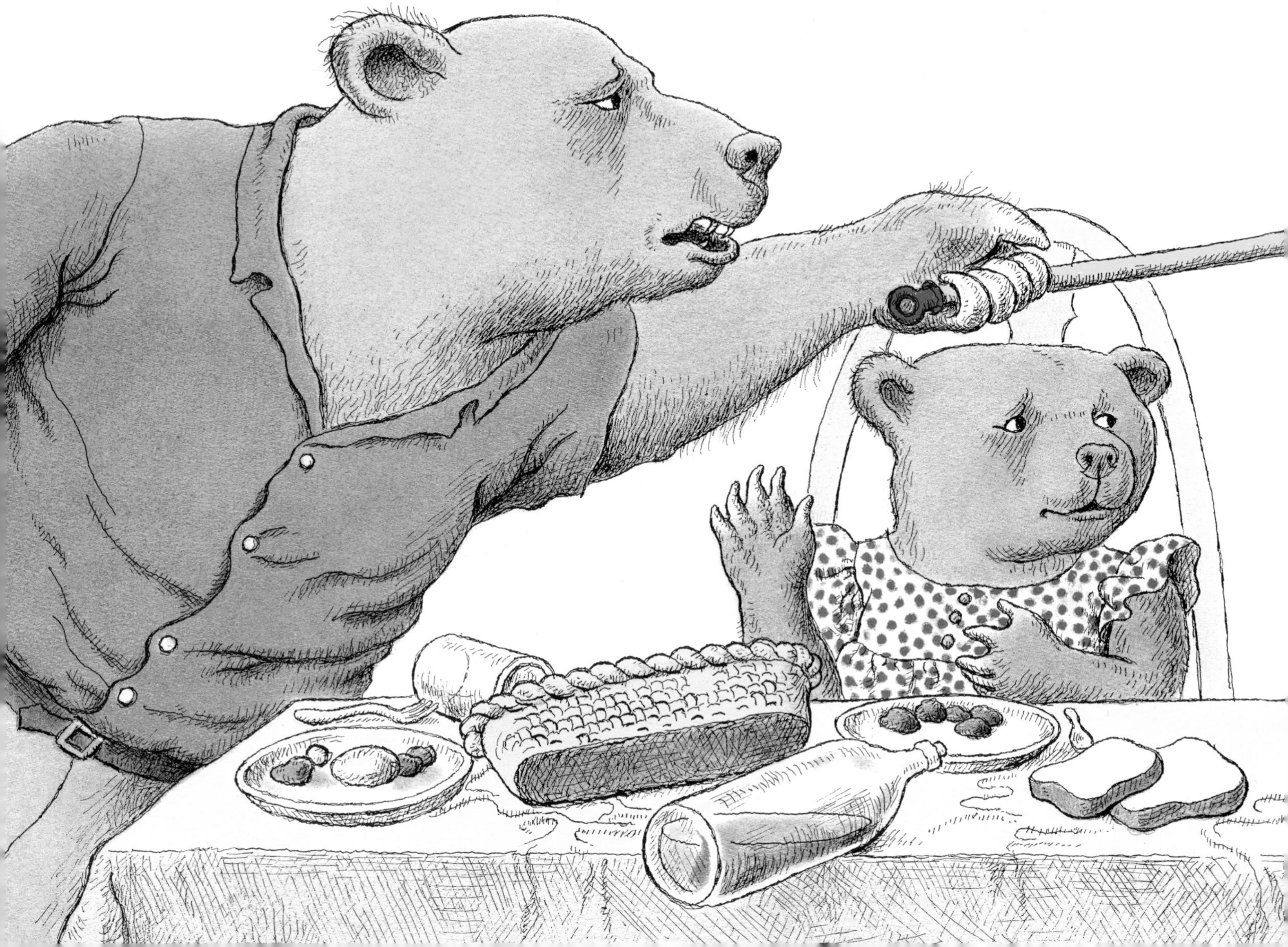

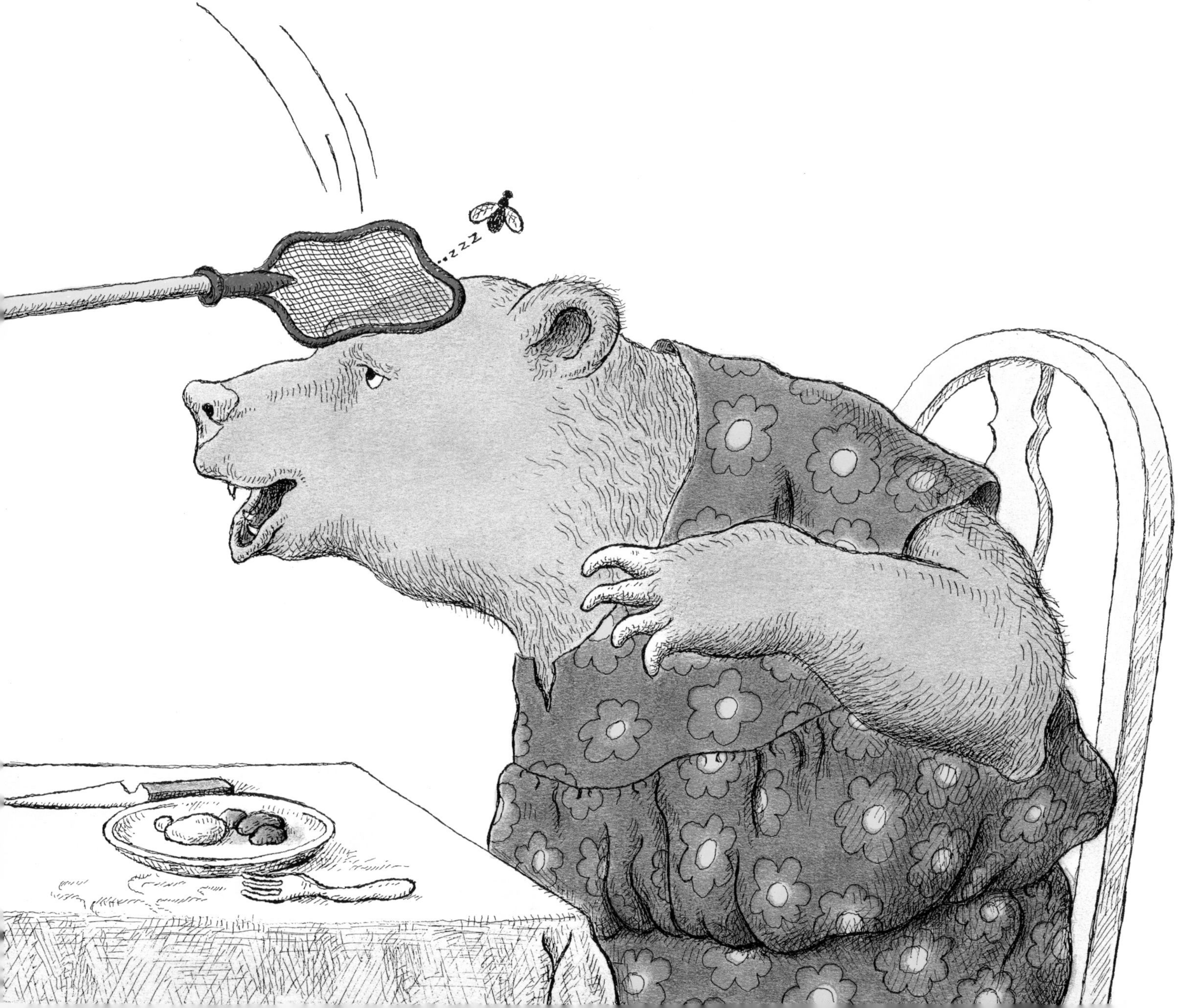
zzzz

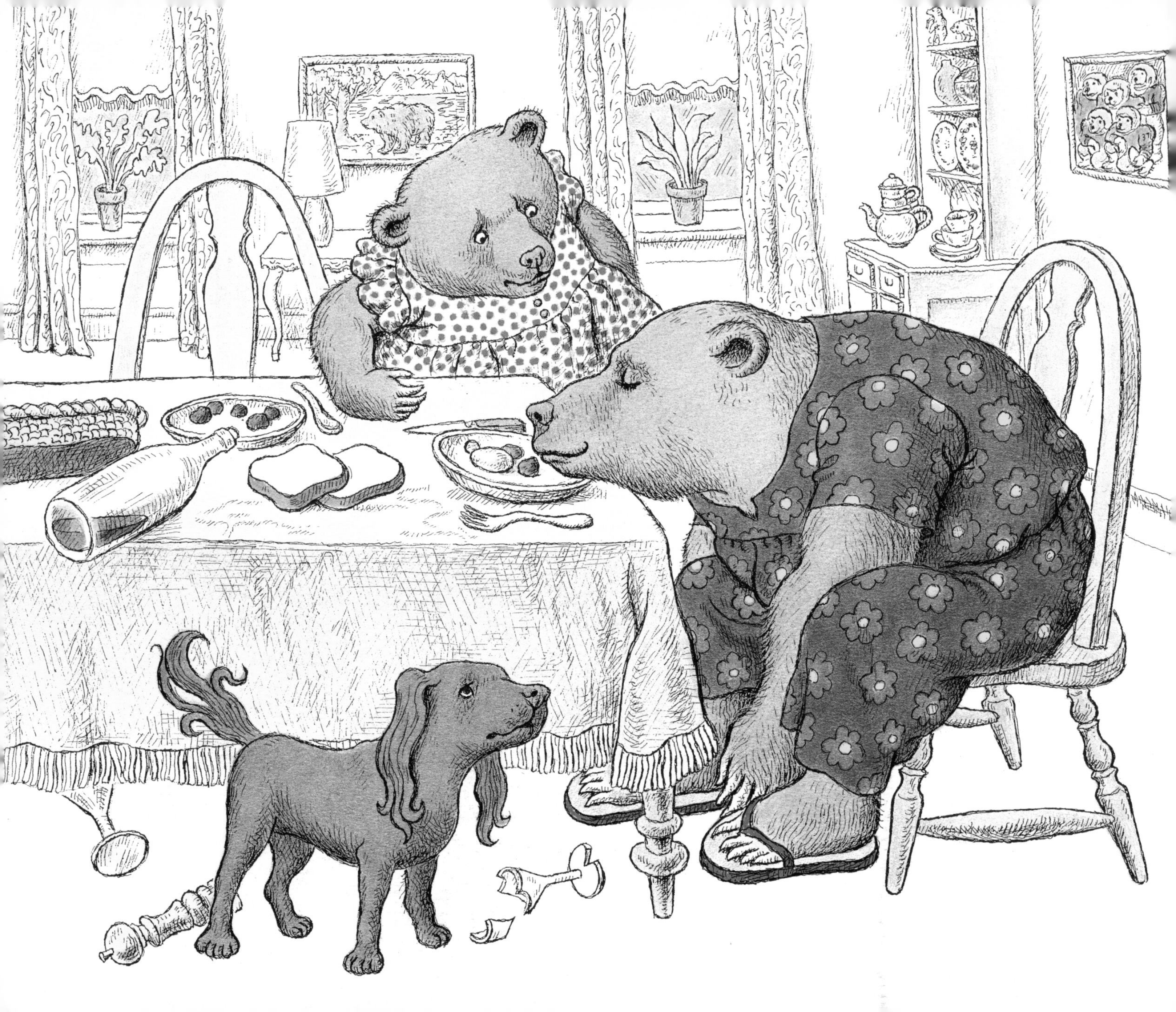

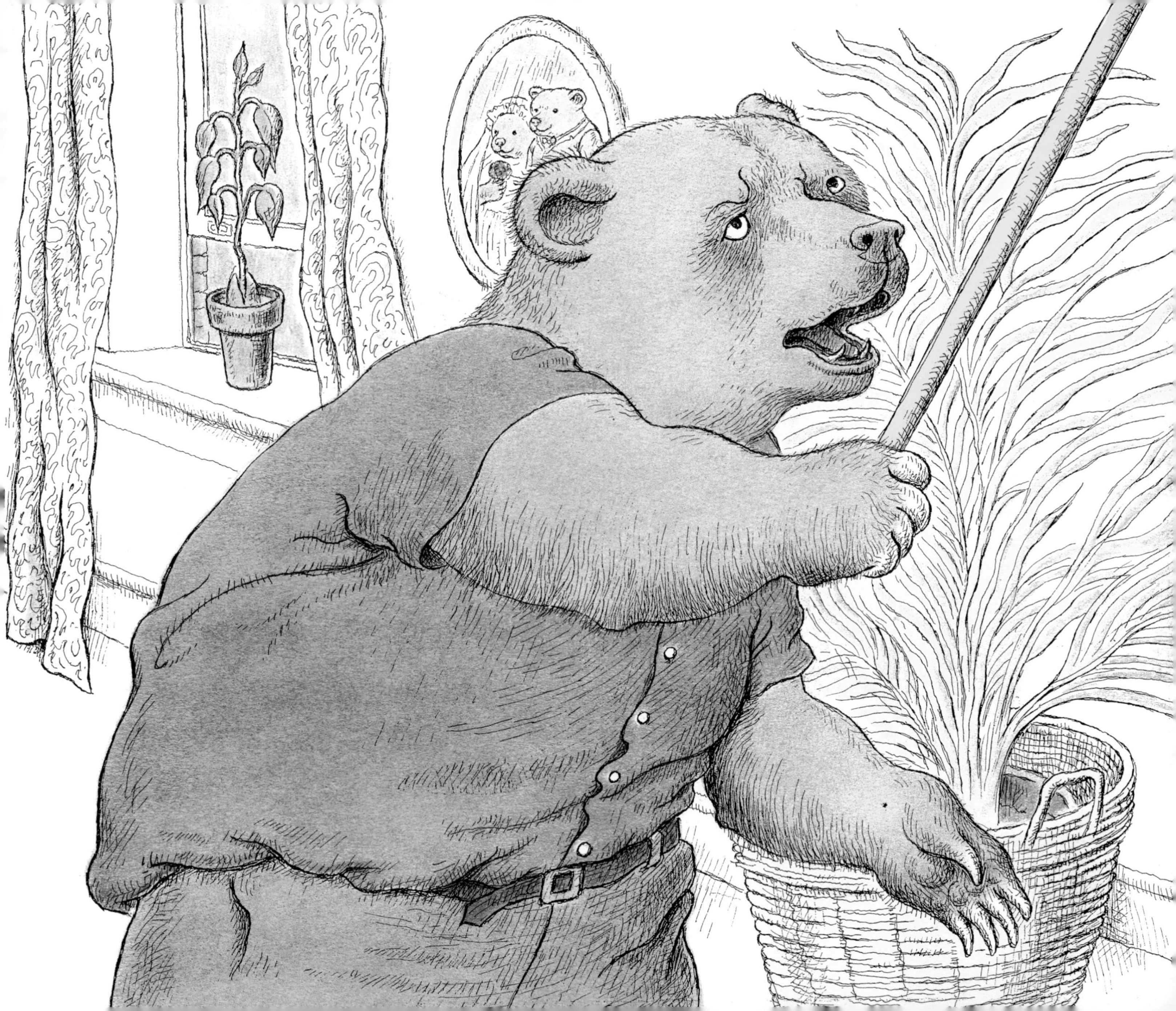

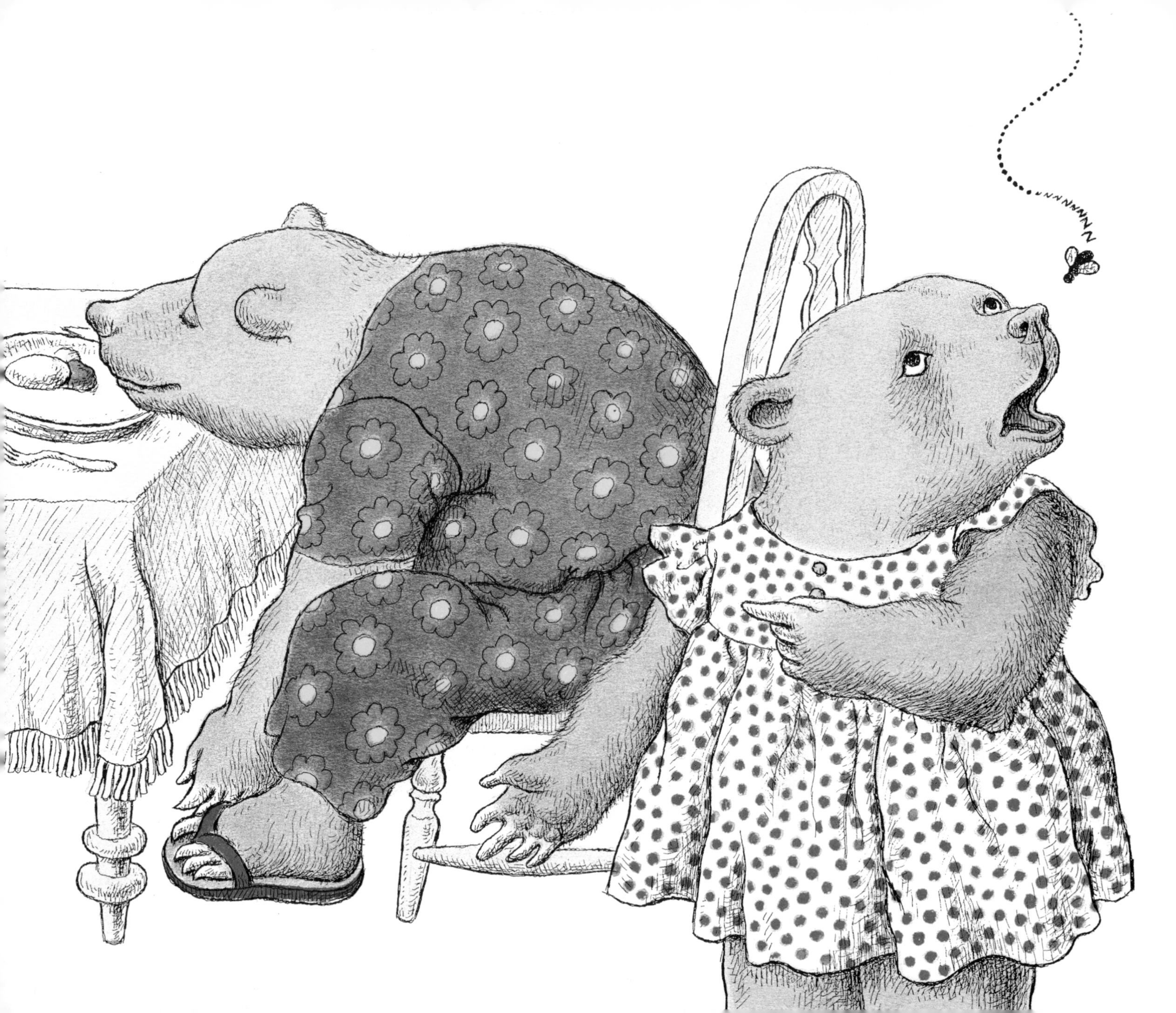

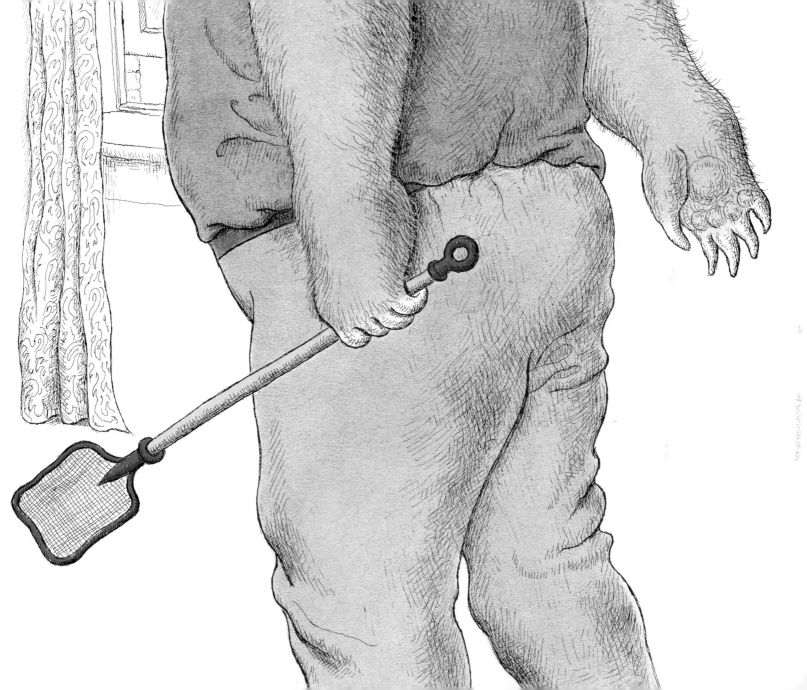

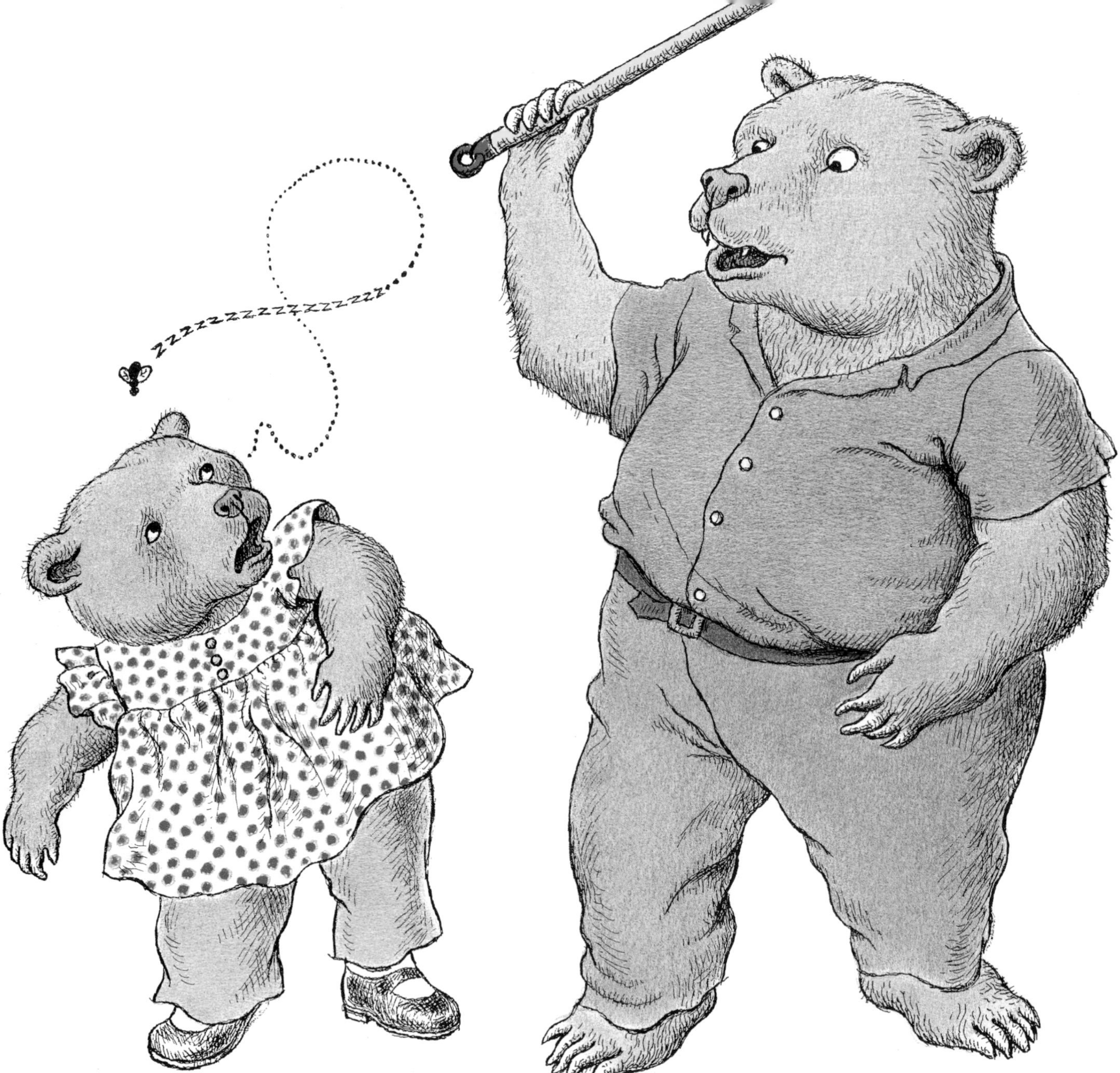

zzzzzzzzzzzzzzzz

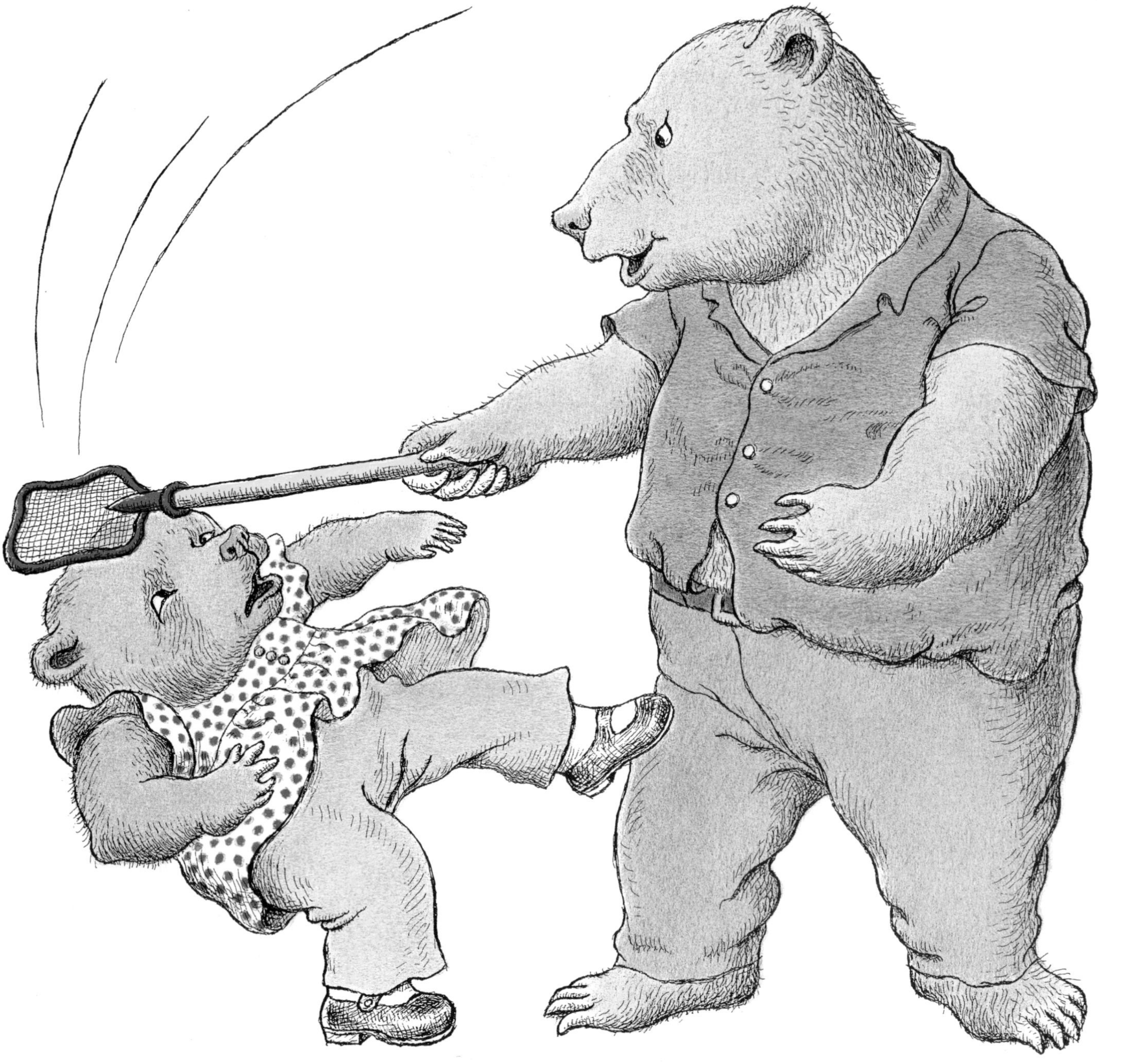

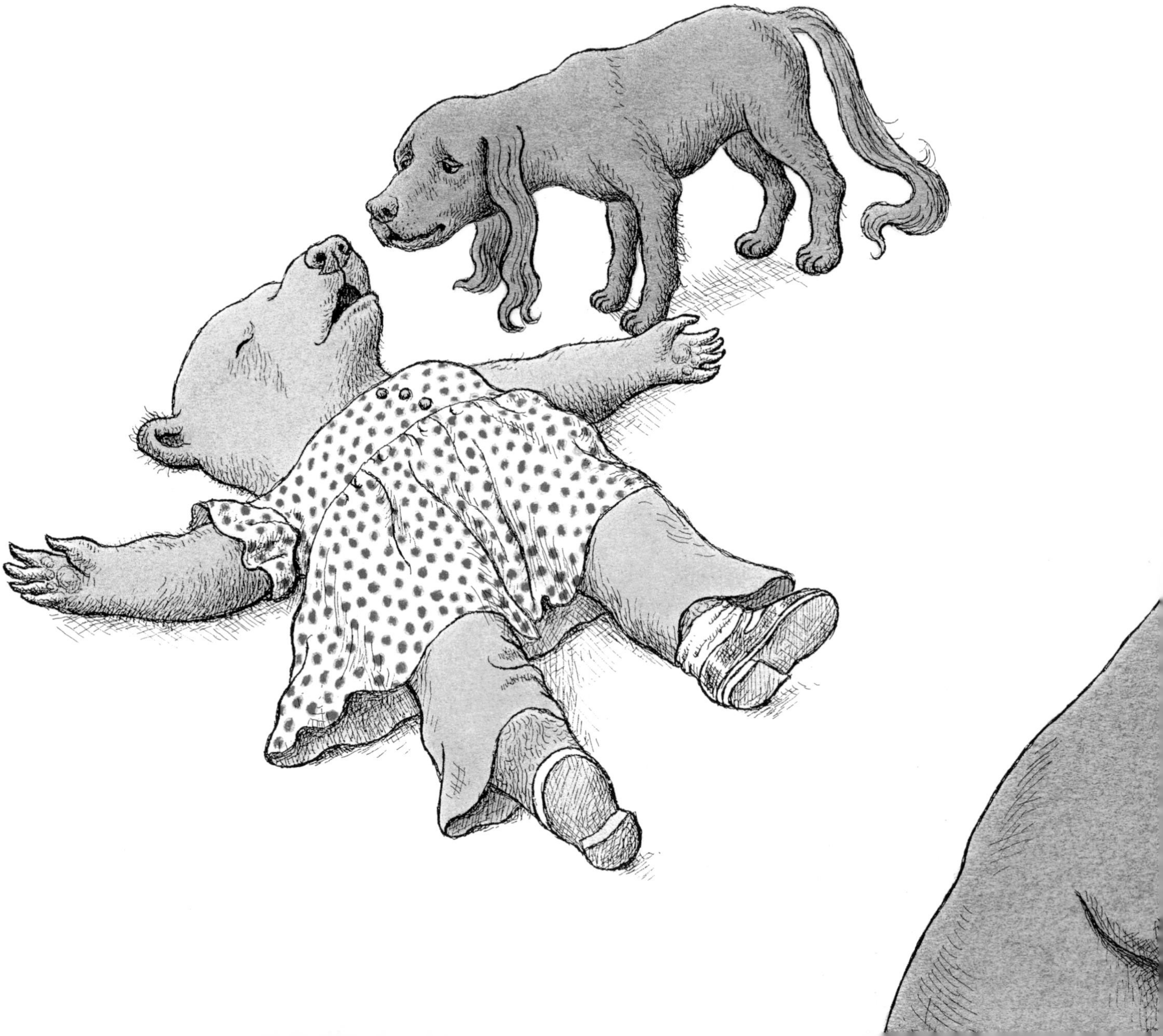

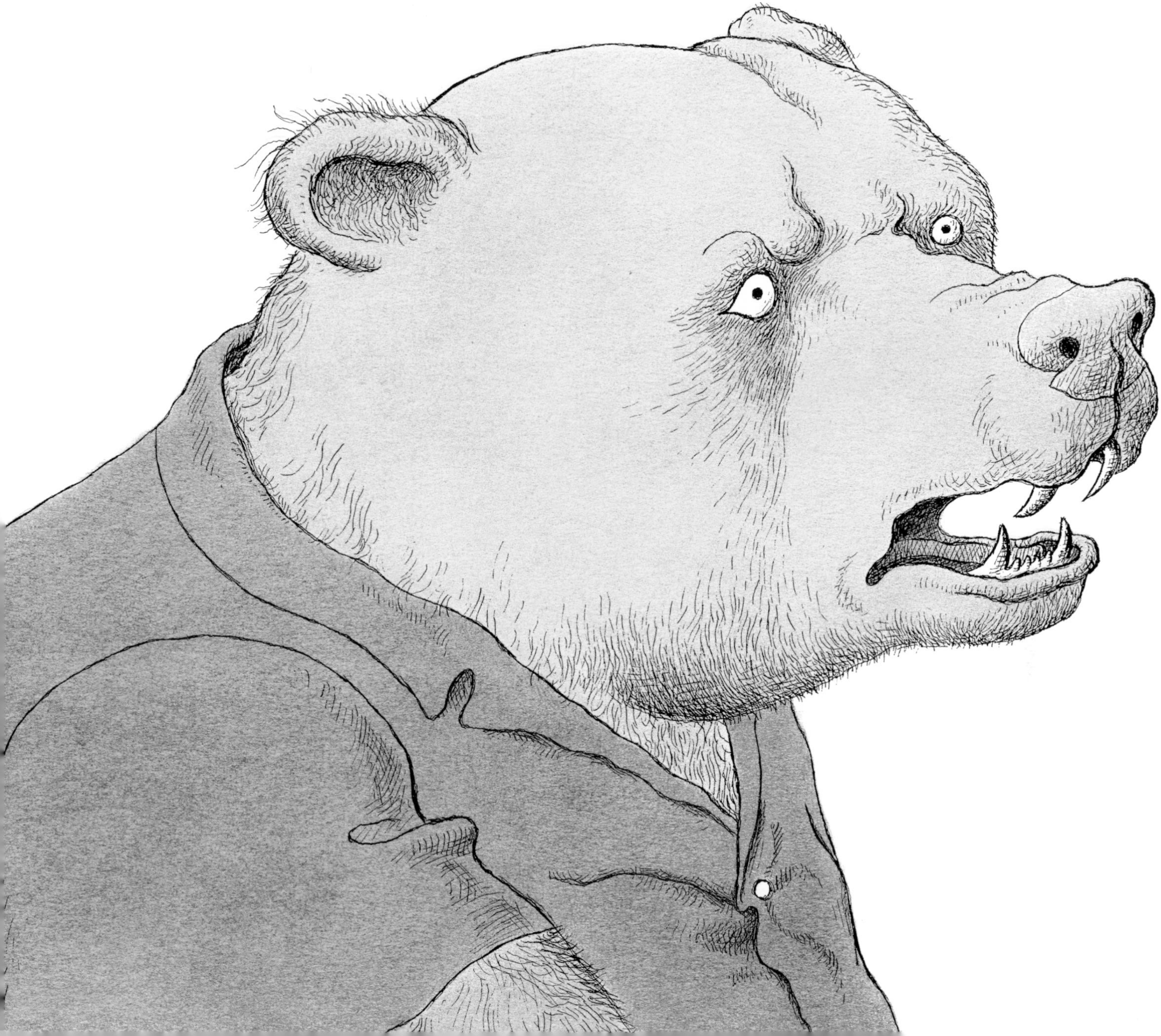

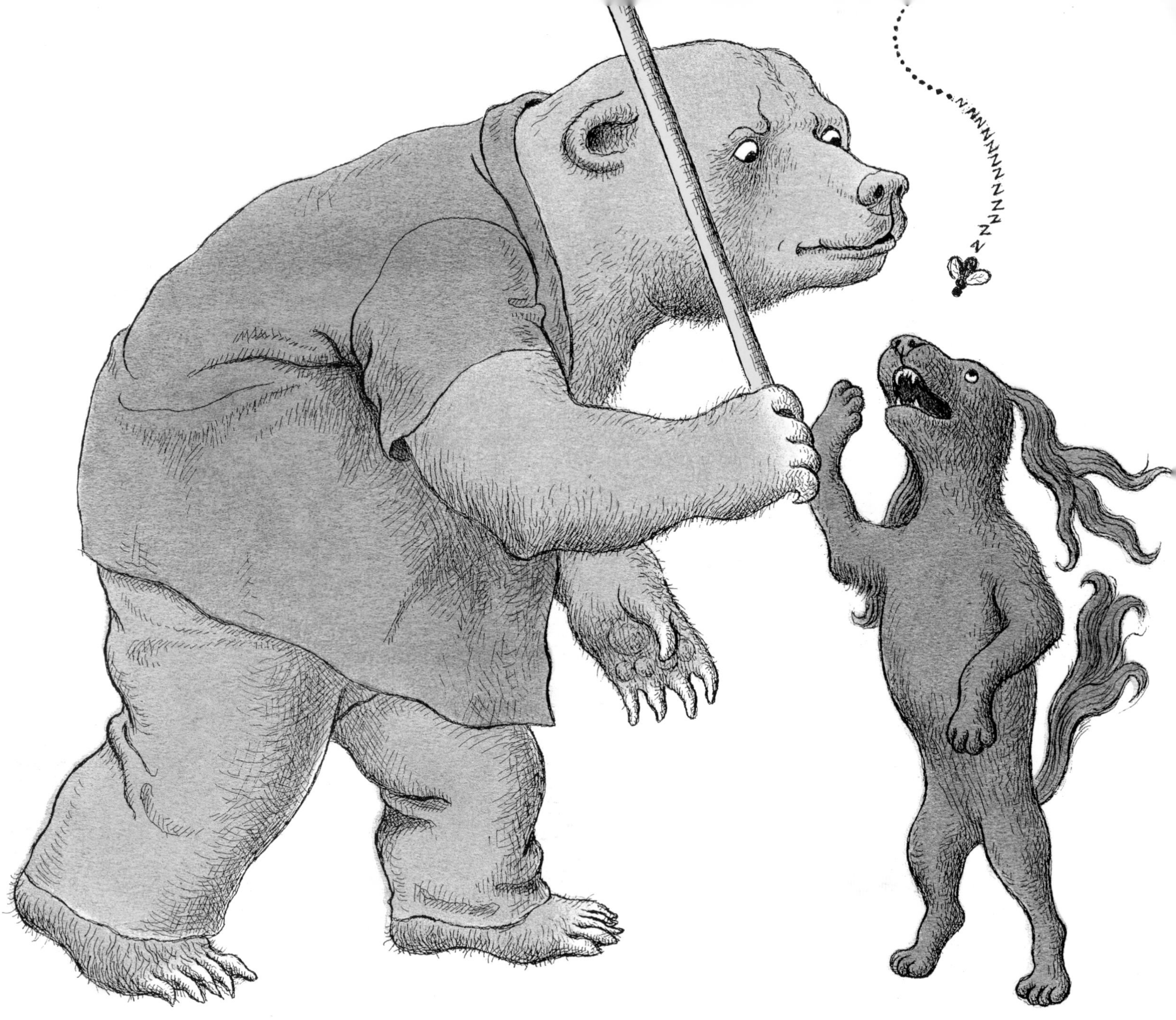

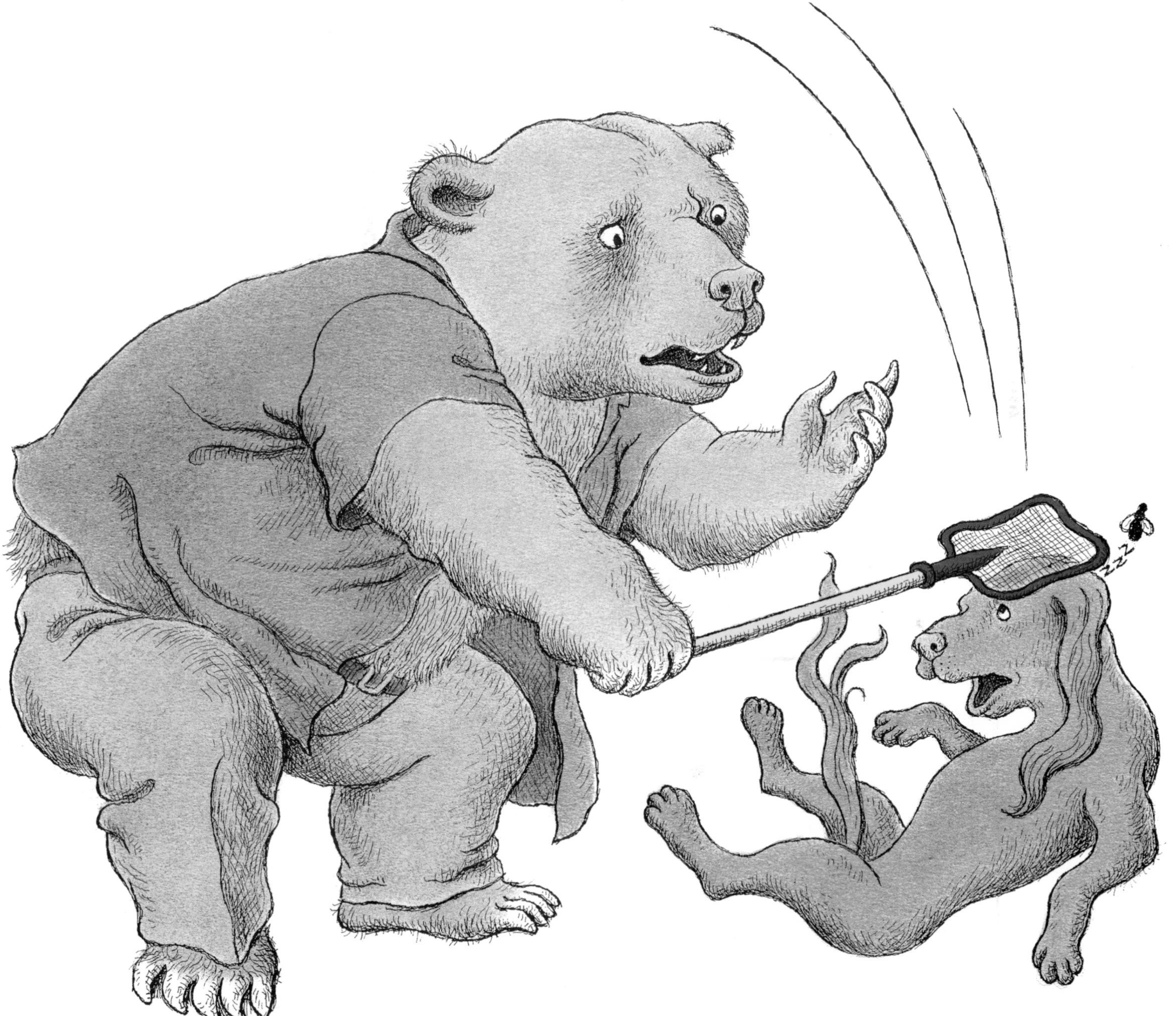
ZZZ

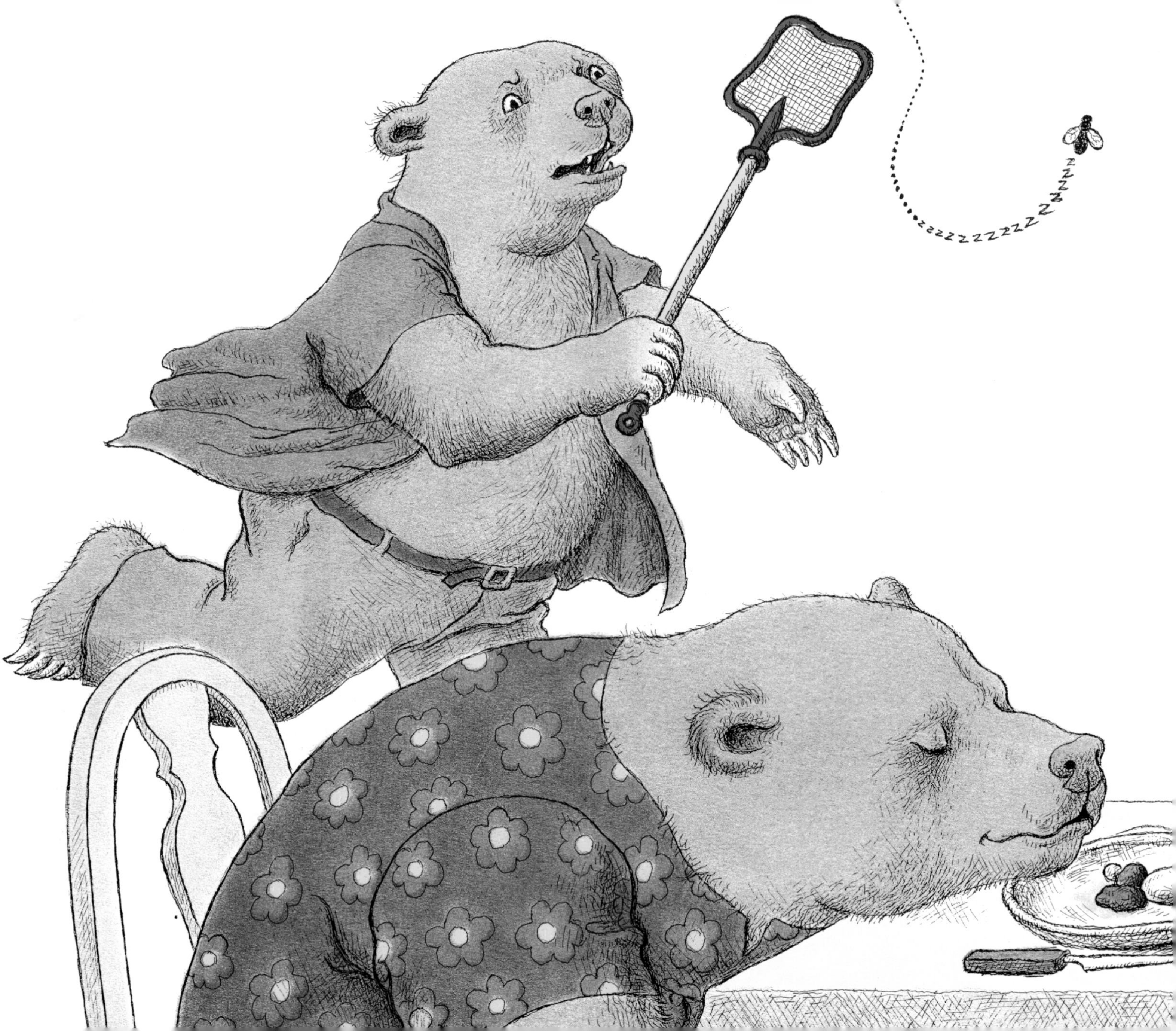

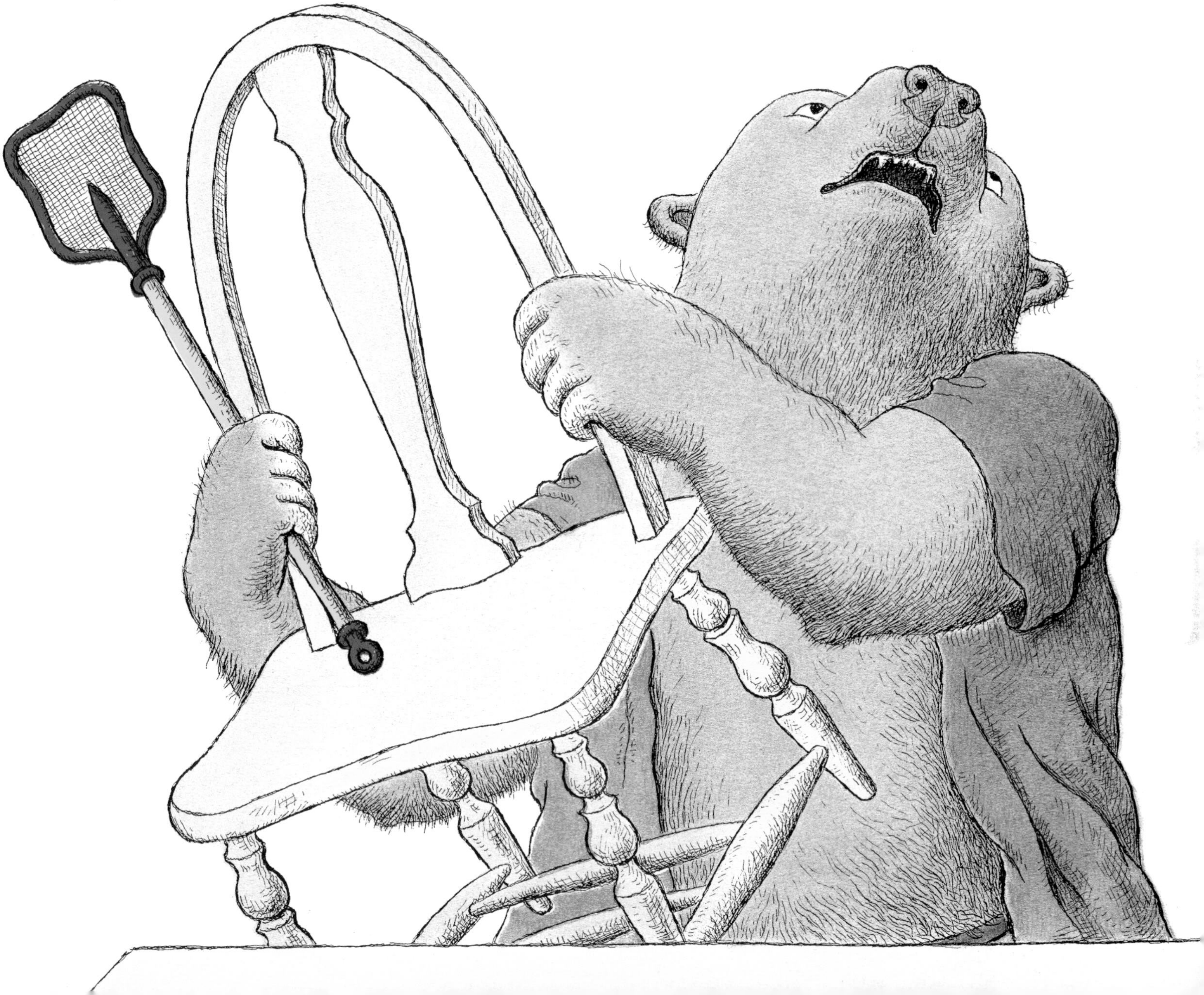

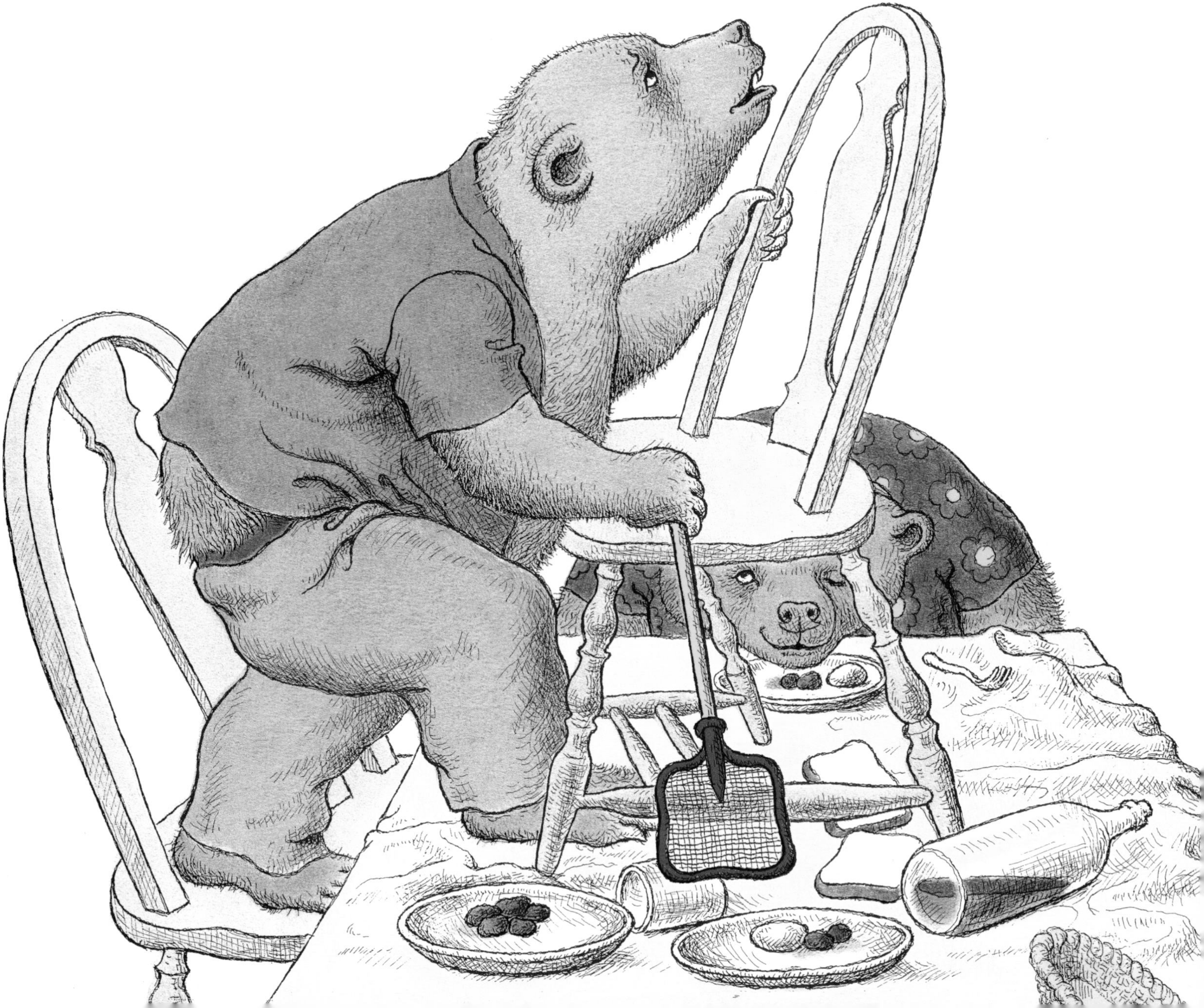

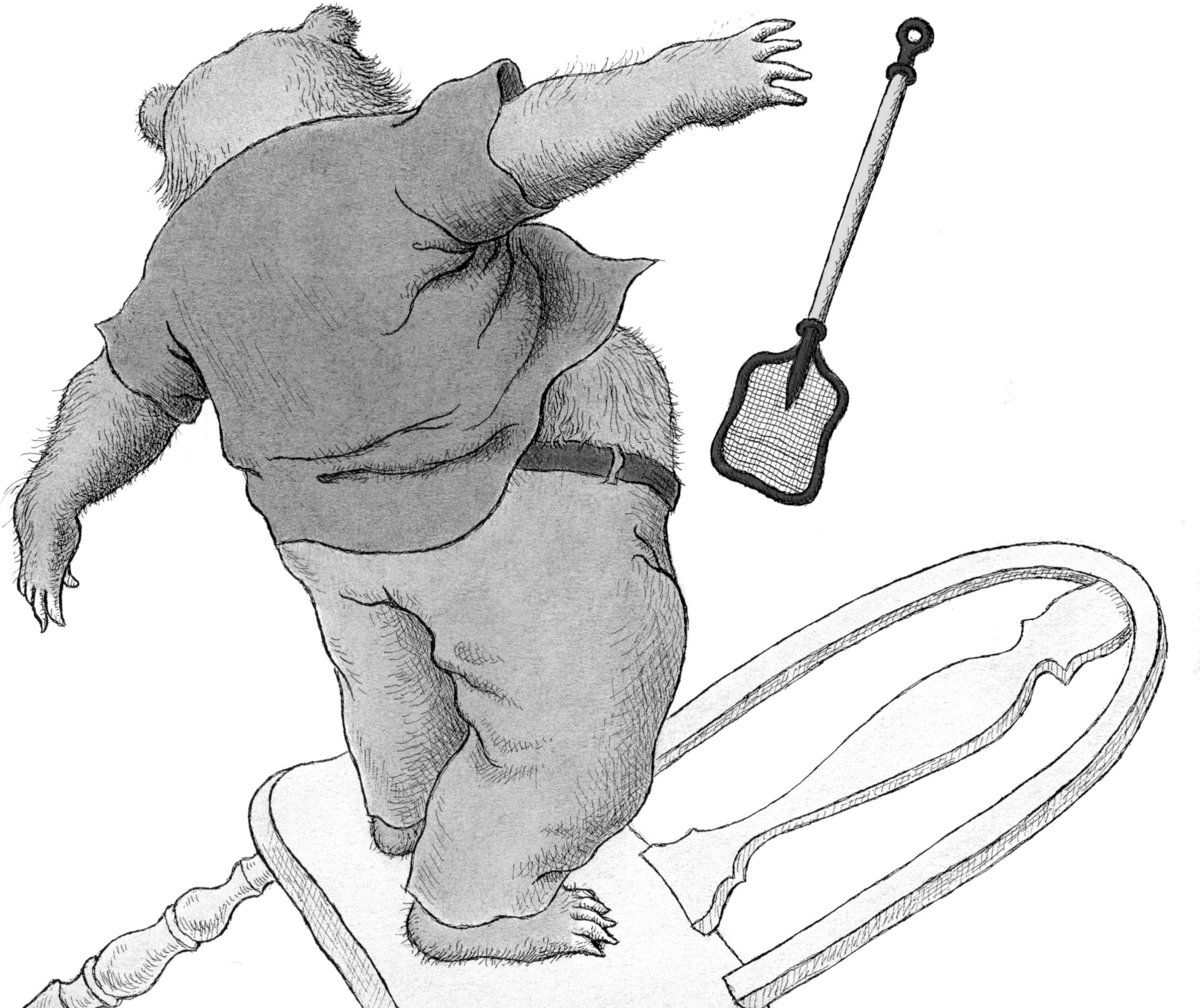

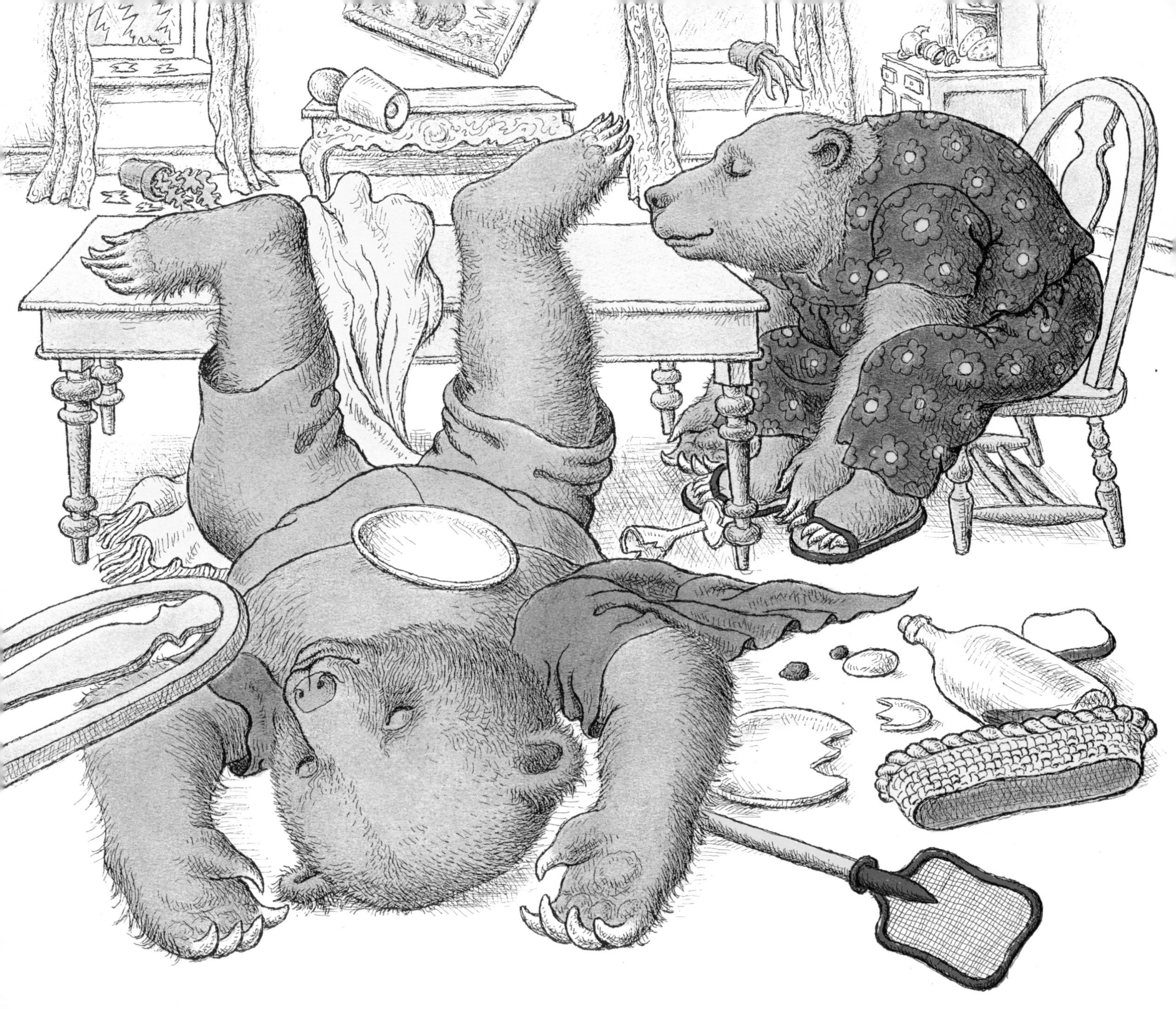

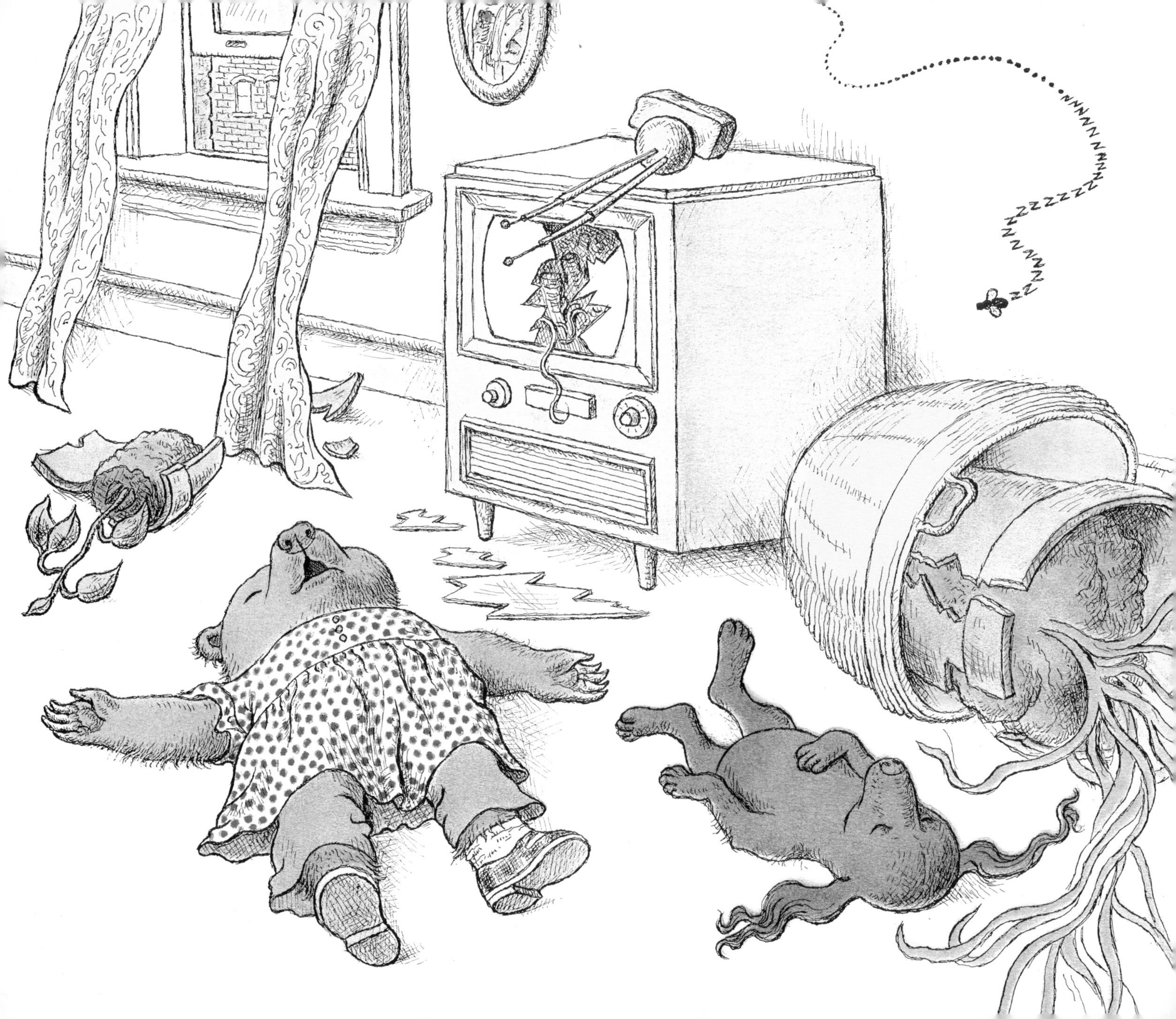

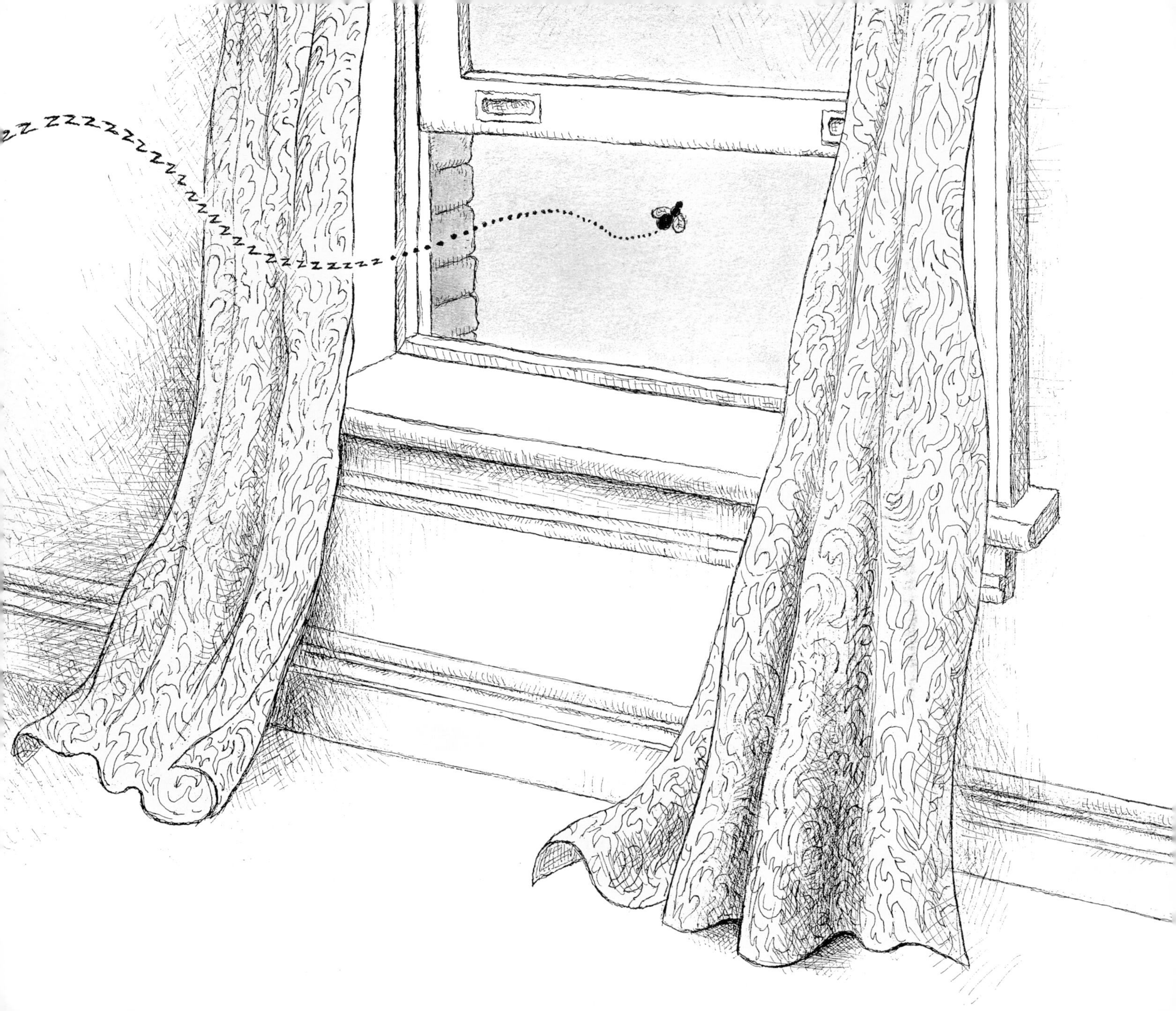